"I think you must be the hairiest monster I have ever seen," says Doreen, one of the hairdressers at the Monster Hair Salon. She stares at the large monster who has just come in. "Your hair is all knotty and even has some bits of stick and rotting food in it," she adds. "You really should take more care of yourself!"

“I don’t like brushing my hair!” whines the hairy monster. “Trying to comb it really hurts, so I don’t bother. My lair is out in the wild, and I don’t often see anyone who would care what I look like. I swim in the lake to clean my hair. I don’t need to do more.”

"The lake does not clean it completely," says Doreen. "Look!" and she holds up a tangled curl of hair and shakes it. "What is this?" she says, pointing to something that looks like a bit of toffee. "Also, your back is covered with sticky weed."

Doreen peels a strand of sticky weed from the monster's back and holds it out to show him.

“Mmmm, sticky weed! Yummy!” says the hairy monster, taking it from Doreen and eating it. “I was eating some of that for breakfast. I found a huge patch by the pear trees. I was going to have pears for breakfast, but then I saw the sticky weed and ate that instead.”

“I picked a load of pears and took them back to my lair. A few were very ripe and squishy and I think some sticky stuff dripped down my side,” he adds, looking at a dirty patch. There were some flies buzzing around it. “Perhaps I do need a shower and a haircut,” he says, sheepishly.

“I took some of the pears to my mother and she told me that I was a disgrace. She said I should make an appointment to see you and get cleaned up. She thinks that I look like a scary monster and that, if anyone sees me, they will run away!”

“Perhaps they will,” smiles Doreen. “Right, let’s start. I think a complete makeover is needed. Take a seat in my chair and we will begin by cutting the sticky bits out of your fur. Then we will clean and trim the rest of it. I’ll dry your hair and you won’t know yourself. Nor will your mother!” she chuckles.

Just then, the door to the salon opens and a spotty, purple monster strolls in.
“Hello, I’m here for my claw cut,” he announces, holding up his right paw. “I broke one yesterday and it needs to be filed and smoothed off. I would also like them polished, as I’m going to a monster party at the weekend.”

“Right,” says Doreen, turning and calling to her assistant, Rue. “Rue! Your next customer is here.”

Rue comes over, greets the spotty purple monster, and shows him to the nail and claw bar.
“Sit in this chair here,” she says, and then sits in the chair opposite and gets out her nail file. She takes the monster’s paw and starts filing down the jagged, broken claw.

"It's hectic in here today," says Rue. "Robert is curling this yellow monster's fur. He's been putting the curlers in her hair since eight o'clock this morning. When they are all in, they have to set, and then I have to help Robert unroll them all. It will look lovely when it is finished," she sighs happily. "Curls all over."

“The twin baby monsters are coming in for their first hair cut at ten o’clock,” continues Rue. “Getting them to sit still in the chair will be the biggest problem! But we have our little monster chair. It’s shaped like a car. The little monsters can pretend to drive along while we cut their hair. It helps to keep them sitting down!”

"Here they are, and here we go!" says Rue, as the twin baby monsters explode into the salon. There is a whirl of arms and noise. The twins are followed by their mother.

"Me first!" shouts one of the twins, rushing over to the car chair. "I'm going to drive the car first!"

“No, me, me!” shouts the other twin, trying to climb up and over into the car chair. Mother monster grabs hold of him, lifts him up, and puts him in one of the waiting room chairs.
“Sit there and wait your turn,” she says sternly.

To the other twin she says, “You sit in the car and sit still so that Milly can cut your hair.”
“Yippee! Broom, broom,” shouts the little monster twin, as he pretends to drive the car chair.

"What a day," sighs Doreen, as she waves goodbye to the twin monsters with their smart haircuts. The spotty, purple monster comes over and shows off his new nail polish.

"Your nails are lovely. Very funky!" says Doreen, as she admires them.

"I cannot wait to show everyone at the party," he says.

“I have just finished here!” calls Robert.
“That looks fantastic. Wow! Very curly!” says Rue, going over to look. “I hope you are pleased?” she asks the yellow monster in the chair.
The monster nods and smiles. “It took a long time, but look at me now!” she says, and twirls around to show off all her new curls.

“And finally,” calls Doreen, “let me show you the biggest change today. Do you remember the dirty, scruffy, hairy monster who walked into the salon this morning? Well, now look!”

The hairy monster creeps shyly into the main salon. His hair is trimmed and styled. There are no sticky weeds or bits of old food. Instead, he has silky, shiny locks.

“You look amazing!” says Rue.

Everyone claps and admires him.

“I’m going to show my mother,” he says, smiling, “and perhaps take her out to dinner!”